FRIENDSHIP
Strawberry Shortcake
CLUB

Secrets and Surprises

By Megan E. Bryant
Illustrated by Laura Thomas

Grosset & Dunlap

Visit www.strawberryshortcake.com to join the
Friendship Club and redeem your Strawberry
Shortcake Berry Points for "berry" fun stuff!

GROSSET & DUNLAP
Published by the Penguin Group
Penguin Group (USA) Inc., 375 Hudson Street, New York, New York 10014, U.S.A.
Penguin Group (Canada), 90 Eglinton Avenue East, Suite 700, Toronto, Ontario,
Canada M4P 2Y3 (a division of Pearson Penguin Canada Inc.)
Penguin Books Ltd, 80 Strand, London WC2R 0RL, England
Penguin Ireland, 25 St Stephen's Green, Dublin 2, Ireland
(a division of Penguin Books Ltd)
Penguin Group (Australia), 250 Camberwell Road, Camberwell,
Victoria 3124, Australia (a division of Pearson Australia Group Pty Ltd)
Penguin Books India Pvt Ltd, 11 Community Centre,
Panchsheel Park, New Delhi - 110 017, India
Penguin Group (NZ), Cnr Airborne and Rosedale Roads, Albany, Auckland 1310,
New Zealand (a division of Pearson New Zealand Ltd)
Penguin Books (South Africa) (Pty) Ltd, 24 Sturdee Avenue, Rosebank,
Johannesburg 2196, South Africa
Penguin Books Ltd, Registered Offices:
80 Strand, London WC2R 0RL, England

Library of Congress Cataloging-in-Publication Data

Bryant, Megan E.
Secrets and surprises / by Megan E. Bryant ; illustrated by Laura Thomas.
p. cm. — (Strawberry Shortcake Friendship Club)
ISBN 978-0-448-44491-8 (pbk.)
I. Thomas, Laura (Laura Dianna) II. Title.
PZ7.B8398Sec 2007
2006024791

10 9 8 7 6 5 4 3 2 1

Chapter 1

Strawberry Shortcake raced down the Berry Trail as fast as she could. The next meeting of the Friendship Club was starting in just a few minutes—and if she didn't hurry, she would be late!

"Hi, everybody!" Strawberry exclaimed as she ran into the Friendship Clubhouse. "Am I late?"

Angel Cake glanced at the clock on the wall. "Only a teeny, tiny, little

 1

bit late," she teased. "But we would never start a meeting without you, Strawberry!"

"Anyway, Ginger Snap isn't even here yet," Blueberry Muffin chimed in.

"Good—that will give me a chance to catch my breath!" replied Strawberry. She grinned at her friends. The kids in the Friendship Club—Strawberry, Angel Cake, Orange Blossom, Ginger Snap, Blueberry Muffin, and Huckleberry Pie—spent time together nearly every day. Once a week, they had a meeting to plan fun things to do. Strawberry never felt happier than when she was with her berry best friends.

As the clock ticked, Angel tapped her foot. "Did Ginger forget about the meeting?"

"No way!" Orange said. "We talked this morning. It's her turn to bring the snack."

Suddenly, the door burst open. It was Ginger Snap!

"Look! Look!" she exclaimed breathlessly, touching her fingers to her head. Ginger's dark hair was pulled back with sparkling barrettes. "They have red ginger flowers on them—my favorite!"

"That's so cool, Ginger!" Strawberry said. "Those clips are berry gorgeous!"

"I *love* them!" squealed Angel. "Where did you get them?"

"I was hoping one of you could tell me," Ginger replied. "I found a package on my doorstep. The clips were inside—but there was no card or note."

"Well, I *wish* I could take the credit," Strawberry said. "But it wasn't me!"

"Me, neither," said Huck.

"Or me," chorused the other kids.

 3

"Then who was it?" Ginger asked.

"I don't know—but it sounds like we've got a mystery on our hands!" Blueberry exclaimed. "Ginger, I *love* solving mysteries! Can I help figure it out?"

Ginger nodded. "Of course!"

"Let's see," Blueberry began. "First we should—"

"Have the meeting?" interrupted Angel. "I want to solve the mystery, too—but we have a lot to talk about."

Blueberry laughed. "Sorry! I guess I got carried away."

The kids sat on the floor in a circle. Ginger set out a tray of cookies.

"We have some berry important business to discuss today," Strawberry announced. "One of our international members, Crêpes Suzette, is coming to visit from Pearis!"

"I can't wait!" Angel cried, clapping her hands together. "Crêpes always knows about the berry latest fashions and styles."

"And we haven't seen her in a long, long time," added Orange.

Strawberry smiled. "I know! I thought it would be really nice if we had a party for her—a surprise party!"

"That sounds *divine!*" Angel exclaimed.

"Raise your hand if you agree," Blueberry said.

All the kids' hands shot up at once.

"Awesome!" cheered Strawberry. "We'll need two kids to make the food, two kids to decorate, and two kids to plan the entertainment. I'd love to cook for the party."

"Me, too!" volunteered Angel.

"I can make decorations," Ginger said.

"I'll help you," Huck offered.

"That leaves entertainment for us, Orange," said Blueberry.

"Sounds good to me!" Orange grinned.

"Great! Let's have another meeting in a few days after we've done some work," suggested Strawberry. "This is going to be the best party ever!"

Chapter 2

After the meeting ended, Strawberry
and Angel walked partway home together.

"I can't stop wondering who left those
beautiful barrettes for Ginger," Angel Cake
said. "She's so lucky!"

"She has a berry good friend, that's for
sure," replied Strawberry. "It's always nice
when someone goes out of their way to do
something special for a friend."

"Absolutely," agreed Angel. "Hey! Maybe

I can plan a surprise for one of our friends!"

"What a great idea!" Strawberry exclaimed. "I'll plan one, too."

"Huck showed me a new way to pitch when we played Berry Ball last weekend," Angel said. "I'll plan a surprise for him."

"Orange was admiring the seedlings in my berry patch yesterday," said Strawberry. "I'm sure she'd love some for her garden."

"Of course she would!" replied Angel.

"You know what else we need to plan?" Strawberry asked. "The food for the party! Want to come over tomorrow morning?"

"Sure! Maybe we can plan some more surprises, too," Angel said.

Soon the girls had reached a fork in the Berry Trail—one path led to Angel's house in Cakewalk; the other led to Strawberryland.

"I'll see you tomorrow morning, then,"
Strawberry said. "Bye, Angel! I can't wait!"

Meanwhile, Blueberry was trying her
best to solve Ginger Snap's mystery.

"The barrettes came in this box,"
Ginger said, handing a small white box to
Blueberry.

"Hmm. Since we've already touched
the box, it will be berry hard to find the gift-
giver's fingerprints," Blueberry said. "Was
there any special wrapping?"

"Plain brown paper," Ginger replied.
"But I already threw it away."

"That's not a good clue," Blueberry
replied. "Everyone can get brown paper."

"It's a mystery." Ginger shrugged.

"Maybe we'll find some clues where you

found the package," suggested Blueberry.

"It was on the doorstep," Ginger said.

Blueberry examined the ground with her magnifying glass. "I'm looking for anything out of the ordinary," she explained.

"Like what?" Ginger asked as she peered at the ground. "It looks like—well, it looks like my front step."

"There could be a hair, or a piece of cloth, or a footprint," Blueberry explained.

"But I don't see anything like that at all," Ginger said.

"Me, neither—no footprints, no fingerprints, no clues," Blueberry said, sighing. "This is a tough mystery."

"But I *really* want to know who gave me these barrettes!" Ginger exclaimed.

"Well, our only hope is that the person

who gave them to you will come forward—
or perhaps leave a clue somewhere else,"
Blueberry replied.

"Thanks, Blueberry," Ginger said. "If
anyone can solve this mystery, it's you!"
Suddenly, Ginger had a great idea—maybe
she could surprise Blueberry with something special to thank her for trying to
solve the mystery! Ginger could hardly keep
a huge grin from spreading across her face.

She couldn't wait to get started!

Over in Orange Blossom Acres, Orange
skipped up the stairs to her tree house. She
was so happy about the party plans that
she almost didn't notice the
package on her doorstep.

Almost.

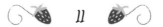

Her heart started pounding as she reached for the package. With trembling fingers, she ripped off the brown paper to reveal a small white box. She flipped open the lid.

Inside was a sparkly ring!

"Oh! It's beautiful!" gasped Orange. "I wonder who it's from!" As she tried on the ring, her brown eyes gleamed happily. "Being surprised is so exciting—now I want to surprise one of my friends!"

Chapter 3

When Strawberry awoke the next morning, the sun was shining brightly. It was another beautiful day—and Strawberry felt her heart leap as she wondered what excitement the day might bring. Right after breakfast, the doorbell rang.

"Woof! Woof! Woof! Woof!"

"Don't worry, Pupcake," Strawberry said to her dog. "It's only Angel Cake."

But Pupcake just barked louder.
"WOOF! WOOF! WOOF!"

"Pupcake!" Strawberry said. "What's gotten into you?" She scooped Pupcake into her arms before opening the door.

But no one was there.

"That's really strange," Strawberry said as Pupcake wriggled to get free.

Then Strawberry looked down.

Two party bags were on her doorstep!

Strawberry gasped. "What's this?" she asked. There was no note on the bags to tell her who they were from.

"Hi, Strawberry! What's that?" called Angel as she walked up the path.

"I don't know," Strawberry replied. "Did you leave them for me?"

Angel shook her head. "How could I

have done that? I just got here," she said. "Plus, there's no way I could have carried one more thing!"

It was true. Angel's backpack was bulging, and she was carrying a large box.

"Then someone must have left me a surprise!" Strawberry said excitedly. She eagerly opened the bags. There was a tiny note card in each bag, one addressed to Pupcake, and one to Custard, Strawberry's cat.

"Custard's bag is filled with tuna-flavored kitty treats," Strawberry said. "And Pupcake's has peanut-butter dog biscuits!"

Pupcake snatched a biscuit out of Strawberry's hand while Custard delicately nibbled on one of her treats. "*Mmm*, tuna snaps," she said, sighing. "My favorite!"

"Anybody who makes my pets happy is a berry special friend of mine," Strawberry declared. "I hope I can figure out who it is!" Then she turned to Angel. "Oh, Angel, let me help you. Your backpack looks so heavy!"

"That's because it's filled with cookbooks," Angel replied. "And the box has a dozen of my special sports cupcakes for Huck."

"Oooh!" Strawberry exclaimed. "Huck's going to love them!"

"I hope so!" Angel said. "I can't wait to pick recipes for the party."

"Neither can I!" replied Strawberry as she put the stack of cookbooks on the table.

The girls flipped through the cookbooks

in silence, placing a sticky note on each page that had a recipe they liked. After they had looked at all the cookbooks, Strawberry turned  to Angel. "Just about every recipe sounds berry delicious—especially this strawberry cake!"

Angel laughed. "I guess we should think about what Crêpes Suzette would like to eat. It might be nice to have her favorite foods in case she's feeling a little homesick."

"Crêpes *loves* cherries," Strawberry said.

"Maybe we should make a cherry tart for dessert," Angel suggested.

"Yes! And let's make crêpes. They're definitely one of Crêpes Suzette's favorite foods," replied Strawberry.

Angel looked confused. "You want *two* desserts?" she asked.

Strawberry giggled. "I was talking about dinner crêpes—the kind that are filled with chicken and cheese and vegetables. Everyone can have a crêpe made with their favorite fillings."

"Oh, I get it!" Angel said excitedly. "We can have a crêpe-making station!"

Soon the girls had a long list of food.

"*Mmm*! Everything sounds berry delicious!" Angel said. "Well, I guess I'll deliver these cupcakes to Huck now."

"I'll come with you," suggested Strawberry. "I can help carry your cookbooks and deliver Orange's surprise, too."

"Oh! Strawberry!" exclaimed Angel. "I almost forgot to tell you—Orange Blossom found a surprise package on her doorstep after the meeting yesterday."

"Really?" asked Strawberry. "What was in it?"

"A shiny ring," replied Angel.

Strawberry grinned. "Well, a tray of baby plants isn't as glamorous as a ring—but I hope she'll like them anyway!" Strawberry opened the door—and was surprised for the second time in one day. A package wrapped in brown paper was on the doorstep!

"I can't believe it!" Strawberry shrieked. "Oh, Angel, what do you think is in *this* package?"

"I don't know," Angel replied. She tried to smile. But inside, she couldn't help wondering why everyone else seemed to be getting so many surprises—and why nobody was leaving any for her.

Strawberry held her breath as she opened the package. Inside were two strawberry-shaped clips attached to shimmering pink hair ribbons. "Oh, they're berry beautiful!" she cried. She pulled her hair back with the clips. "Aren't they the berry best ribbons ever?"

"Definitely," Angel said, trying to sound more excited than she felt. "Come on, Strawberry, let's go. I have a lot of stuff to do today."

As they walked along the Berry Trail, Strawberry was chattering so excitedly that she didn't notice how quiet Angel had grown until after they had dropped off the surprises for Huck and Orange. Strawberry wasn't quite sure what was wrong with Angel. She didn't know that, as they walked up to Angel's house, her friend was eagerly searching her front porch for a package.

But there was nothing there. Angel couldn't help sighing.

"Is everything okay, Angel?" Strawberry asked. "You seem kind of sad."

"Oh, I'm fine," Angel said quickly. She didn't want to tell Strawberry how disappointed she was that no one had left a surprise on *her* doorstep. "Really. I'm just a little worried about, um, how hard some of those recipes look."

"You have nothing to worry about!" exclaimed Strawberry. "You're one of the best cooks in all of Strawberryland."

Angel looked into Strawberry's kind brown eyes and felt better about everything. "Thanks, Strawberry," she said, giving her a hug.

"No problem," Strawberry replied. "If you feel worried again, call me! I know we can do it." With a little wave, Strawberry set off for home.

Angel was embarrassed about feeling jealous of all of Strawberry's surprises. She knew that Strawberry was a great friend to everyone she met—of course they would want to surprise her with special presents! And suddenly Angel wanted to do something nice for Strawberry, too. She thought about how much Strawberry loved strawberry cake. A smile spread across Angel's face as she planned the very next recipe she'd make: a strawberry cake for Strawberry Shortcake!

Chapter 4

Blueberry Muffin had read so many mystery books that she knew a lot about looking for clues and cracking cases. And there was something about the Strawberryland mysteries that didn't make sense. Some of the surprises looked identical from the outside: white boxes covered in brown wrapping paper. But the other surprises were wrapped in colorful paper. Blueberry was starting to think that there was more than one person involved in this mystery. But how many? And *who*?

When the phone rang, she had a feeling it would be about another surprise.

And she was right!

"Hrumph Blumblerry!" A boy's muffled voice came through the receiver.

"Huck? Is that you?" Blueberry asked, trying not to giggle. There was a pause before the person replied.

"Yup, it's me!" Huck said. "Sorry, Blueberry. You answered the phone before I could swallow this giant bite of cupcake!"

"That sounds yummy!" replied Blueberry.

"It's the best," Huck said. "And the cupcakes are why I'm calling. I figured out who's been leaving the surprises!"

"Who?" Blueberry asked excitedly.

"It's Angel Cake!" Huck said. "I found two packages on my doorstep. One had a new baseball cap in it. And the other had my favorite sports cupcakes! They taste just like the ones Angel makes—so it must be her."

"What?" shrieked Blueberry. "You're *eating* the evidence? Don't eat another bite, Huck! I'm coming over to look for clues!"

And before Huck could reply, Blueberry hung up the phone and ran out the door. When she reached Huck's fort, Blueberry examined the scene. The kitchen floor was littered with a pastry box, a blue ribbon, a white box, and brown wrapping paper. A tray of cupcakes—one missing several large bites—sat on the table. And the crisp new hat was already on Huck's head.

 25

"Do you see any clues?" Huck asked.

Blueberry shook her head. "There aren't any clues left," she explained. "I assume that the cupcakes were in the pastry box with the blue ribbon? And the hat was in the white box with the brown paper?"

"Yeah!" Huck said, impressed. "How'd you know?"

"It follows the pattern of the other surprises," said Blueberry. "Angel probably did leave the cupcakes, Huck. But I don't think she's been leaving the brown-wrapped packages that keep popping up."

"But both packages were waiting for me when I got home," argued Huck. "I think Angel left the cupcakes *and* the hat. I can't wait to thank her! I'm going to plan a really special surprise! Don't tell Angel, okay?"

"I won't tell anybody," promised

Blueberry. "But all of these surprises are getting berry confusing!"

"I know," replied Huck. "Want a cupcake?"

"*Mmm*, that's delicious," Blueberry said as she took a bite. "It does taste just like Angel's vanilla cake."

"I know—because Angel is the one who left the surprises!" teased Huck. "It's getting dark. Want me to walk you home?"

"Sure!" Blueberry replied.

Huck and Blueberry split another cupcake while they walked to Blueberry Valley. As they approached Blueberry's house, Blueberry stopped. "Is there something on my door?" she asked.

"It looks like a piece of paper. Or an envelope!" Huck said excitedly. "Do you think it's a surprise?"

"Let's find out!" Blueberry said.

There was a rustling in the berry bushes. Suddenly, a figure dashed across the path!

"*Ahhhhhhhhh!*" Blueberry screamed.

"Don't worry, Blueberry!" Huck hollered. "I'll catch him—or her—or whoever it is!"

Huck dashed off after the mysterious person, with Blueberry following behind him. But the figure disappeared before they could catch up.

"It's no use," Huck finally said. "I don't see anybody. Sorry, Blueberry."

"That's okay," Blueberry said. "We may have lost the suspect, but the clues are back at my house!"

"Can I help solve the mystery?" asked Huck.

"Sure, Huck!" Blueberry said. "But don't touch anything, okay? We don't want to contaminate the evidence!"

Back at Blueberry's house, she put on some rubber gloves from her detective kit and examined the envelope with a magnifying glass.

"Do you recognize the handwriting?" said Huck.

Blueberry shook her head. "I think they tried to disguise their handwriting—see how they printed in big, capital letters? That's a sure sign," she explained.

Next Blueberry shook dark brown powder over the envelope. She used a soft makeup brush to dust away extra powder.

"What are you doing now?" asked Huck. "And what's that stuff?"

"This is cocoa powder," Blueberry

explained. "If there are fingerprints on the envelope from the person who touched it, the cocoa powder will stick to them. Then we'll be able to see the prints." Once again, Blueberry pored over the envelope with a magnifying glass.

Her sigh told Huck that she didn't see a single print.

"What next? When are you going to open the envelope?" Huck asked impatiently.

Blueberry laughed. "Now, I guess," she replied. Inside the envelope was a stack of pages covered in words and drawings.

"It's—it's a story!" she exclaimed. "It's a story about a world-famous detective named Blueberry Muffin! Oh, Huck, I think someone wrote this story about *me*! I can't wait to read it!"

"But don't you want to check all

those pages for fingerprints?" Huck asked.

Blueberry paused. "Well," she said slowly, "kind of. But if I pour cocoa powder on them, I'll ruin the drawings. It might make it hard to read parts of the story. And whoever made this for me went to an awful lot of trouble. I'd hate to ruin all their hard work—even if it does mean I have to give up on this mystery." She was silent for a moment. "You know, Huck, I think I'll use the cocoa powder to make some hot cocoa. Would you like a cup? If you want to hang out, I can read the story aloud!"

Huck grinned. "I love cocoa," he said. "I want to find out what happens to Detective Blueberry Muffin!"

"And besides," Blueberry added, "I don't think we've seen the last of these mysterious surprises—which means there will be plenty more clues to find!"

Chapter 5

The next afternoon, Strawberry called her friends to remind them about the upcoming Friendship Club meeting. Huck and Ginger weren't home, so Strawberry left messages for each of them. Then Strawberry called Blueberry Muffin. "Hi, Blueberry!" she said cheerfully. "I was just calling to see how the entertainment plans are going for Crêpes Suzette's party."

"Oh!" Blueberry exclaimed. "I, um . . .

oh, Strawberry. I sort of—um—I forgot all about it!"

"You *forgot*?" Strawberry asked. "How could you forget? This is the biggest project the Friendship Club has ever tried to do!"

"I know," Blueberry replied miserably. "I'm really sorry. I've just been so busy trying to solve all the mysteries! Please don't be mad, Strawberry."

"I'm not mad," Strawberry said gently. "I'm just a little worried. We have so much to do, and Crêpes will be here in four days."

"I'll call Orange right now so we can start planning," said Blueberry.

"Thank you," Strawberry said. "I'll see you tomorrow, okay? And would you remind Orange about the meeting for me?"

"Definitely!" Blueberry promised. "Bye, Strawberry."

Strawberry called Angel Cake next.

Brrring! Brrring! Brrring!

"Hello?" answered Angel.

"Hi! It's Strawberry. You didn't forget about the Friendship Club meeting tomorrow, did you?"

"Of course not!" Angel replied.

"Oh, good," Strawberry said, relieved. "I'll see you at the clubhouse at two o'clock."

"You got it, Strawberry," Angel said. "And don't be surprised if I bring a little *surprise* with me!"

"A surprise? What are you—"

Click!

Angel had hung up!

Strawberry smiled. "Now that I've reminded everyone about the meeting, I need to figure out what I'm bringing for a snack," she said. "I know! I'll make a strawberry cake, like that recipe Angel and I found. Everyone loves cake—and I love strawberry cake berry, berry much!"

Strawberry wasn't the only one planning to make a strawberry cake. The very next morning, Angel Cake woke up early. She was so excited about baking a special cake for Strawberry that she stopped wondering why no one had planned a surprise for her.

"I already know exactly what's going to happen when I give Strawberry the cake!" Angel said to her pet lamb, Vanilla Icing. "She'll be so surprised. And she will absolutely *love* the cake. Of course she'll offer cake to everybody else, and they'll all love the cake, too! And everyone will tell me what a good job I did!"

Angel measured and mixed all the ingredients for the cake. Then she poured the batter into two pans and put them in the oven.

"Time to slice the strawberries and make the frosting!" Angel sang out.

Two hours later, Angel Cake stood back and examined the cake. "This is the berry best cake I've ever made!" Angel said proudly. "I think I have enough time to get some ingredients for the party food before the meeting. Take care of the cake, Vanilla Icing!"

Angel skipped out the door. She was so pleased with herself that she didn't notice Huck hiding in a lollipop tree!

As soon as Angel was out of sight, Huck snuck into her house. "Hi, Vanilla Icing," he said. "I'm here to do something really nice for Angel—clean her kitchen! It's the least I can do since she made me those awesome cupcakes!"

Huck started sweeping, scrubbing, mopping, and dusting. Soon the kitchen was sparkling.

"Just one more thing to do— clean off the tops of the cupboards," Huck said. He carefully climbed onto the counter. Standing on his toes, he was just able to reach the very tops of the cupboards.

Suddenly, Huck started to lose his balance. "Whoa—oh—oh!" he yelled as he slipped and fell—right into the strawberry cake!

"Oh, no!" Huck yelled as Vanilla Icing ran and hid. "Look at this mess! Angel's kitchen looks worse than it did before I started cleaning!"

Huck was right. Chunks of cake, globs of frosting, and bits of strawberries were *everywhere*—even on the ceiling. And Huck was covered in cake, too!

"I can't believe I wrecked the kitchen *and* the cake," Huck muttered. "Now I have to clean everything again. Angel's gonna be so mad at me!"

Huck went right to work cleaning up the mess. When he was finished, the kitchen was sparkling once again. "Come out, Vanilla Icing," he called. "Everything's okay. I promise I won't be smashing any more cakes today."

Shyly, the little lamb peeked into the kitchen. It looked beautiful—completely clean from bottom to top.

"I guess I should leave Angel a note explaining what happened to the cake," Huck said reluctantly. "But if I do that, it will ruin the surprise of her nice, clean kitchen. Maybe she won't even notice that the cake is missing! I can explain everything—and apologize—when I see her at the Friendship Club meeting." Suddenly Huck looked at the clock. "Oh, no! The meeting starts in ten minutes! Bye, Vanilla Icing—I'm sorry I scared you and made a giant mess!" Huck zipped out the door and ran off to Huckleberry Briar.

A few minutes later, Angel Cake hurried into her house, carrying two heavy bags of groceries. "Oh, I hope Strawberry won't be mad that I'm late to the meeting," she worried. "I just have time to put these groceries in the fridge, get the cake, and—"

Suddenly Angel stopped. She stared at the empty counter.

"Where's the cake?" Angel asked slowly. "Vanilla Icing! Where's the beautiful cake I spent all morning making?"

But Vanilla Icing just stared at Angel with big, sad eyes.

"What could have happened to it?" Angel asked. "I've got to find that cake!"

Angel searched her whole house for the cake, but it was nowhere to be found. "I *know* that cake was on the counter when I left!" she exclaimed as she started to cry. "Someone must have stolen that beautiful cake I made for Strawberry! And I—I—I *promised* I was bringing a surprise to the meeting! Oh, she's going to be so disappointed when I show up with—with—with *nothing*! I know what it feels like when your friends don't even bother to plan a surprise for you!"

Angel buried her head in Vanilla Icing's fleece and sobbed. Finally she dried her eyes and took a deep breath. "I still have to go to the meeting," Angel said bravely. "I just hope Strawberry will understand when I tell her what happened to her surprise."

Chapter 6

At the clubhouse, Strawberry was watching the clock impatiently. She barely listened as Blueberry described the second surprise she'd found—a shiny blueberry-shaped locket wrapped in brown paper.

"The meeting should have started fifteen minutes ago!" Strawberry finally exclaimed. "Where are Huck and Angel?"

"I'm sure they'll be here soon," Orange said.

"Maybe we should begin without them," suggested Ginger Snap.

"I guess we'll have to," Strawberry said, sighing.

"This meeting of the Friendship Club will come to order, even though two of our members are late," Ginger announced. "Who wants to talk about their plans for Crêpes's party?"

"Maybe Blueberry and Orange should go first," suggested Strawberry, "since our partners aren't here yet."

"Okay," Ginger replied. "Go ahead, guys!"

"Well, we didn't start planning the entertainment until this morning," Blueberry said. "But once we got together, we had a lot of great ideas! I'm making a CD that has the top songs from Pearis and from Strawberryland, so we'll have a really cool mix of music. And Orange—well, I'll just let Orange tell you herself."

Orange grinned. "I thought maybe we could put on a fashion show," she said shyly. "I know that Crêpes loves everything about clothes."

"That's perfect!" Strawberry said. "And we can wear our fashionable new accessories—the surprises we all received."

"But Strawberry—Angel hasn't gotten one," Blueberry said quietly.

Strawberry frowned. "That doesn't make any sense," she said. "Why would everyone get a surprise except for Angel?"

Her friends just shrugged and looked away.

"Well, we won't wear our accessories if Angel doesn't get one," Strawberry said.

"But the party is still three days away—that's plenty of time for Angel to get one."

"For me to get what?"

Strawberry looked up to see Angel standing in the doorway. Her face was red and streaked with tears.

"Angel, what's wrong?" Strawberry asked, jumping up. "You look so upset!"

"Oh, Strawberry, it's just *terrible*!" Angel choked back a sob. "I spent all morning making a surprise for the meeting, and it *disappeared*! It was mostly for you, Strawberry, but I knew everyone would enjoy—" Angel's voice trailed off. She stared past Strawberry.

"Where—where did *that* come from?" Angel asked, her voice trembling as she pointed at the strawberry cake.

"I made it!" answered Strawberry.

Angel stared at Strawberry in disbelief. How could this be happening? Why would Strawberry try to pass off the cake as her own? Suddenly all of Angel's shock and disappointment turned to anger. Her blue eyes were icy. "*I* made that cake, and you stole it!" she yelled.

The color drained from Strawberry's face. "What are you talking about?" she asked. "It was my turn to make a snack for the meeting, so I made a strawberry cake."

"Strawberry Shortcake, that is *not* the truth!" Angel cried. "I made that cake this morning and it *disappeared* from my house when *you* stole it!"

Ginger stood up. "Angel Cake, Strawberry isn't a liar or a thief," she said firmly. "You need to apologize to her right now."

"How do you know, Ginger?" snapped Angel. "Can you prove she didn't take it?"

"Can you prove that she did?" Ginger shot back. "You better calm down, Angel, because you're acting like a big baby."

Angel was silent. Then she tossed her golden hair. "I won't stand here and be insulted," she said coldly. "Go ahead and take *her* side. I don't care." She spun around on her heel and stormed out.

For a moment, no one spoke. Then Strawberry said in a shaky voice, "I don't really feel like having the meeting anymore. I'm going home."

"Strawberry, wait—" Blueberry said.

But Strawberry just walked away.

"Well, this is a huge mess!" Ginger said angrily. "I don't believe that Strawberry stole that cake. No way!"

Orange sighed. "You know how Angel gets carried away," she said.

Blueberry shook her head. "But that's no excuse. You can't call your friend a liar and a thief. That's just wrong. Maybe I should go over to Angel's house to see if I can solve the cake mystery. I could look for clues."

"Look for clues? Has there been a new surprise?" Huck asked as he ran into the room. "Sorry I'm late! Hey—where is everybody?"

"Oh, Huck, you just missed the worst fight in the history of Strawberryland!" Blueberry burst out. "Angel accused Strawberry of stealing a cake she made!"

Huck's mouth dropped open. "Oh, no," he groaned. "This is all my fault!"

"How is it *your* fault?" asked Ginger.

Huck sighed. "Did Angel even mention her nice clean kitchen?"

The girls shook their heads.

"I went over to Angel's house to surprise her by cleaning her kitchen," Huck explained. "But I slipped and fell onto this big cake she made. It looked like that one." Huck pointed at Strawberry's cake. "So I cleaned up the mess, went home to change, and then came to the meeting. I was going to tell Angel what happened when I saw her."

"But Angel just jumped to conclusions when she saw the cake that Strawberry made," realized Orange. "And now she and Strawberry are really upset!"

"Huck, go explain what happened to Angel," Ginger said. "Then bring her to Strawberry's house when she's ready to apologize. Blueberry and Orange, let's go see

Strawberry. She must be feeling berry sad right now."

"Okay, everybody," Huck said. He took a deep breath. "I'll go talk to Angel. Wish me luck!"

Chapter 7

A few minutes later, Huck knocked on Angel Cake's door.

"Go away, please," she called in a sad voice. "I don't want to see anyone."

Huck knocked louder. "Angel, it's Huck. I really need to talk to you!"

Finally, the door opened. Angel seemed to forget that she wanted to be alone when she saw her friend. "Oh, Huck! I have to quit the Friendship Club!" she cried. "I just had the biggest fight ever with Strawberry and Ginger because—"

"Angel," interrupted Huck, "I ruined your cake."

Angel stared at Huck. "What?"

"I snuck into your house this morning because I wanted to clean your kitchen," Huck continued. "You know, as a surprise. The only problem was that I slipped and fell—right in that beautiful cake you made! I cleaned up the mess and decided to tell you all about it at the Friendship Club meeting. But that was wrong—I should have told you about smashing the cake when it happened. Or at least left you a note." Huck looked down at the ground. "I'm really sorry, Angel. I only wanted to do something nice for you."

Angel clapped her hands over her

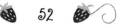

mouth. "Oh, Huck!" she said, horrified. "I thought—there was a strawberry cake at—you mean Strawberry really did make that cake?"

Huck nodded.

"I made a terrible mistake!" Angel cried. "I have to find Strawberry—*right now!*"

She ran so fast down the Berry Trail that Huck could barely keep up. Her heart was pounding as she knocked on Strawberry's door.

When Strawberry opened the door, she looked surprised to see Angel—but she didn't say anything.

"Strawberry," panted Angel. "I'm so—so—so sorry." She paused to catch her breath, and Strawberry opened the door wider so that Angel could come in.

Ginger, Blueberry, and Orange sat quietly on Strawberry's couch as Angel walked into the room.

"I was so upset that I wasn't thinking straight," Angel tried to explain. "I saw the cake and it looked just like the one I made—so I thought—"

"But how?" Strawberry asked. "How could you ever think that I would steal your cake and pretend that I made it?"

"It doesn't make any sense at all!" Angel said, shaking her head. "I've been feeling pretty bad lately," she continued in a soft voice. "Everyone's gotten a surprise—except for me. But I guess I didn't deserve one. I'm not a berry good friend at all."

"Actually, Angel," Huck spoke up, "I

think you did get a surprise. It was on your doorstep—but you were running so fast to get to Strawberry's house that you didn't see it." He held out a package wrapped in brown paper.

But Angel just shrugged. "The surprises don't seem important anymore," she replied. "They're not nearly as important as being a good friend. When I figure out how to do that, I'll open the package."

"Angel Cake, you *are* a good friend," Strawberry said. "But you do get carried away sometimes. You should know that I would never take something that didn't belong to me—or lie to you!"

"I do know that," Angel said quietly. "If you give me another chance, I promise I won't get carried away like that ever again. At least, I'll *try* not to get carried away."

Strawberry gave Angel a big hug. "Deal!" she said. "Now would you *please* open that package? We're all wondering what's inside it!"

Angel Cake slowly removed the brown paper. Inside the box was a pair of shimmering rosebud earrings. "They're wonderful!" she whispered.

"And they're going to match your favorite hat perfectly!" Blueberry said.

"Does anyone still want to have the Friendship Club meeting?" Orange asked.

"Sure," said Strawberry. "But let's stop planning surprises until *after* the party."

"Fine with me," Blueberry said quickly.

"Me, too," added Angel. "Now let's go back to the clubhouse so that everyone can have a piece of that beautiful cake Strawberry made!"

The next three days were a whirlwind of
activity as the friends got ready for Crêpes
Suzette's visit. Strawberry and Angel spent
two whole days cooking together. Huck and
Ginger built a runway for the
fashion show and decorated
the clubhouse with balloons
and streamers. Blueberry and
Orange spent hours making
special CDs.

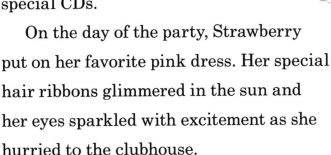

On the day of the party, Strawberry
put on her favorite pink dress. Her special
hair ribbons glimmered in the sun and
her eyes sparkled with excitement as she
hurried to the clubhouse.

Her friends were already there, wearing
their new accessories. "Hi, Strawberry!"

cried Blueberry. "I'm so excited!"

"I know!" Strawberry replied. "I can't wait until Crêpes gets here!"

"What are we going to do to pass the time?" asked Ginger.

"We could try to figure out who the surprises were from," suggested Blueberry.

"Well, everyone knows that I'm the one who cleaned Angel's kitchen!" Huck announced. As the other kids laughed, Angel started blushing. "And I think Angel's the one who made those awesome cupcakes for me," Huck added quickly.

"You're right!" Angel said.

"I never figured out who made the treats for Pupcake and Custard," Strawberry said.

"It was me," Orange said. "But I thought you knew because you dropped off some plants for me that afternoon!"

Strawberry laughed. "What a funny coincidence—I surprised you, and you surprised me on the same day!"

"Okay, so who wrote me that story?" asked Blueberry.

For a moment, no one spoke. Then Ginger said, "I did! I wrote it! I did a lot of research to make sure the mystery made sense. I even used some of the things I learned to make sure I didn't leave any clues. And then you almost caught me when I was dropping off the surprise!"

"So you were the one running away from us!" exclaimed Huck.

Blueberry grinned. "Good work, Ginger. I *knew* the surprises were all from different people!" she said proudly. Then her face fell. "But I still never figured out who gave us all those amazing accessories."

"For the last time, who sent them?" Ginger asked.

Then Blueberry's eyes grew wide. "Wait a minute," she said. "Everyone in this room has a special accessory—so no one here could have sent them!"

"Then *who* did?" asked Strawberry.

Suddenly, the door burst open. *"Bonjour! Bonjour!"* It was Crêpes Suzette!

"SURPRISE!" yelled the kids as they ran to hug her.

"Ah, zis is wonderful!" Crêpes said in her charming Pearisian accent. *"Merci, merci!* And I see zat you are all wearing ze accessories I sent—*très bien!"*

"Wait—you sent them?" Blueberry exclaimed. *"You?"*

60

"Ah, *oui*, of course,"
Crêpes replied. "I sent zem
ahead, by butterfly mail. I did not
want zem to be crushed in my suitcase.
Zey are ze latest style in Pearis!"

"Butterfly mail," Blueberry said to
herself. "No fingerprints, no footprints—
no wonder I couldn't find any clues!"

Strawberry started to laugh. "Thank
you, Crêpes! We love them!" She linked
arms with her friend. "And we have a few
surprises for you. Just wait until you see
what we've been doing!"

"Yeah!" yelled Huck. "Let's get this
party started!"

Strawberry grinned as everyone filed
outside for the fashion show. It wasn't a
secret or a surprise that she had the berry
best friends around!

WE TRAIN WRITERS

Mentor-Guided Email Courses For Youth And Adults

Courses • Conferences
Contests • Critiques

JERRY B. JENKINS
CHRISTIAN
WRITERS
G U I L D

ChristianWritersGuild.com
ContactUs@ChristianWritersGuild.com
Toll-Free (866)495-5177

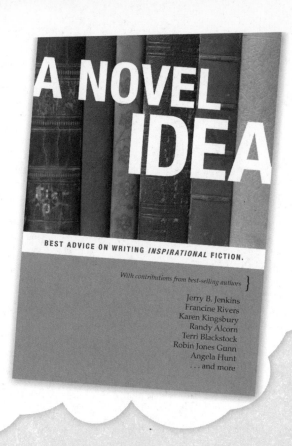

A NOVEL IDEA

BEST ADVICE ON WRITING *INSPIRATIONAL* FICTION.

With contributions from best-selling authors }

Jerry B. Jenkins
Francine Rivers
Karen Kingsbury
Randy Alcorn
Terri Blackstock
Robin Jones Gunn
Angela Hunt
. . . and more

Expert advice from successful fiction writers who have published thousands of novels, with more than 70 million copies sold.

Whether you're a novice or have been writing for years, learn the best ways to plan, perfect, and promote your writing. Discover what makes a novel Christian, and master the art of writing about tough topics.

This valuable guide contains tips on

> plotting,
> dialogue,
> point of view,
> characterization,

> marketing,
> social networking,
> and more. . . .

For the first time, best-selling Christian novelists have joined together to bring you this comprehensive guide on the craft of writing. If you've always wanted to write the next great novel or felt compelled to tell the story that's burning inside you, *A Novel Idea* will give you the tools you need.

CP0373